The Skinny Elephant

Frankeisha Stutts

Frankeisha Stutts

ISBN-10: 153722073x

ISBN-13: 978-1537220734

DEDICATION

To my nieces, nephews, god son, and all the children of the world…

May you always be comfortable and confident in who you are and know Whose you are.

Love you

Once upon a time
there was an elephant
named Skinner.

You couldn't find an
elephant with legs
any thinner.

He loved to play
soccer everyday.

He was so fast the other
elephants couldn't keep up,

when they would play.

Jackie and her brother Bonner were Skinners biggest fans so they visited everyday!

As his popularity grew,
crowds of people would
gather...

to see the skinny elephant
named Skinner.

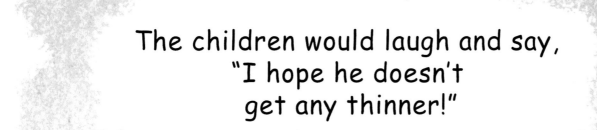

The children would laugh and say,
"I hope he doesn't
get any thinner!"

Skinner never noticed he was different you see.

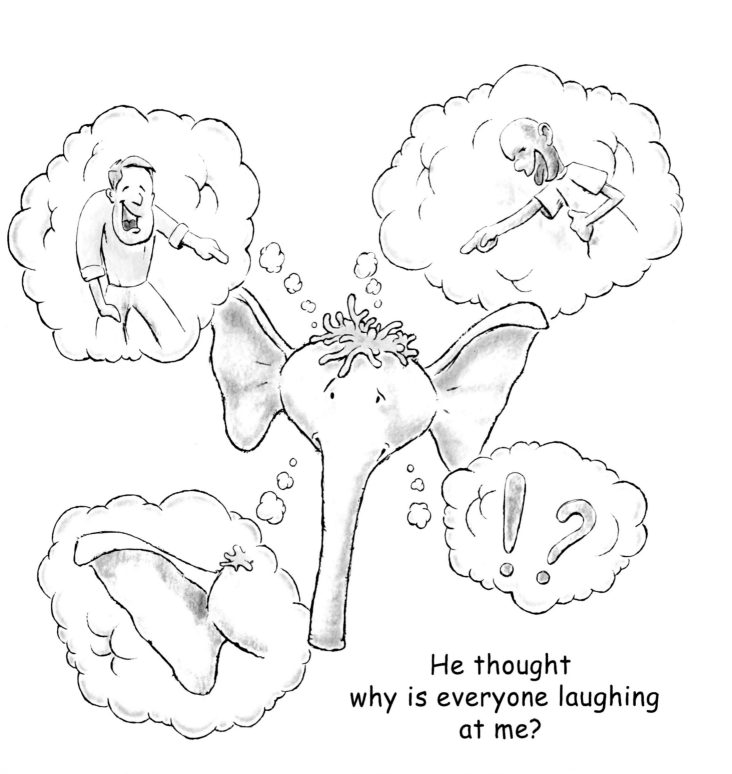

He thought
why is everyone laughing
at me?

Skinner looked
at the other animals
to compare.

He thought
why don't the children
laugh at them and
stare?

He saw two lions with their huge paws.

He saw three giant brown bears
with their long claws.

Skinner looked at four
giraffes with long necks
standing so tall.

He felt like he was
the only animal at the zoo
that didn't fit in at all.

Skinner thought if he could look like the other elephants,

people wouldn't laugh at him.

So he ate and ate, but
still he stayed slim.

Skinner hid in the corner
and tucked his trunk
hoping not to be seen
at all.

Jackie and Bonner knew
something was wrong.
They yelled "Skinner,
where is your ball?"

Skinner began to think of ways to escape from the zoo.

He wanted to find a place he would be accepted with his fuzzy hair and skinny knees too.

He planned carefully and decided to break out after the zookeepers took him for his bath that night.

So
when the night came
and the timing was right,

Skinner made his
escape and darted
out of sight.

He ran past the two
lions as quiet as he
could be.

He ran past the three
bears hoping they
would not see.

He even ran past the
four giraffes they
didn't see him flee.

Skinner exited the zoo

and now he was free.

Life outside the zoo
was a big contrast.

His heart was beating
so fast as all the cars passed.

He spotted a path
along the road and
followed it as quiet as
a mouse.

Skinner didn't know it but, it was the path to Jackie and Bonner's house.

Jackie was so excited
to see Skinner her
feet barely touched
the ground.

He was happy to see Jackie too. Skinner thought what a happy place I've found.

Jackie and Bonner
never laughed at
him whatsoever.

Bonner even gave
Skinner his soccer
ball so they could play
together.

While Skinner played, he noticed that Jackie and Bonner didn't look the same at all.

One was short and
one was tall. One was big
and the other
was small.

Skinner learned from the kids that being different was great!

He said, "I love my skinny snout."

He walked
with his trunk
up in the air.

The kids were overjoyed
and started to dance
and shout.

He was having so much fun playing with Jackie and Bonner too.

He felt safe with them,
but missed his friends
back at the zoo.

Skinner returned to
the zoo bubbling with pride,
as he strutted
past the other animals
inside.

Sometimes the children still laughed and were unkind.

Skinner ignored the children because he knew he was divine. His look came from the Creator and that made him feel perfectly fine.

ABOUT THE AUTHOR

Frankeisha Stutts is a whimsical child author.
Her first manuscript of *The Skinny Elephant* was written
as a fourth grader. She developed a love of elephants
and other animals from her yearly trips to the zoo. Later,
she revised the book to reflect a stronger central
character. She is the proud aunt of two nephews and
three nieces. Frankeisha Stutts currently resides in
Dallas, Texas.

ACKNOWLEDGEMENTS

With deepest gratitude and appreciation, I humbly give thanks to all my friends and family who helped to make this book a reality.

To my mom, Ruth Stutts Moseley, I would like to thank you for keeping my book all these years. I could not have completed this book without your love and support.

To my illustrator, Graeme Rushing, I couldn't have brought Skinner to life without you. Thank you for seeing my vision and bringing it to the pages of *The Skinny Elephant.*

Made in the USA
Middletown, DE
17 December 2016